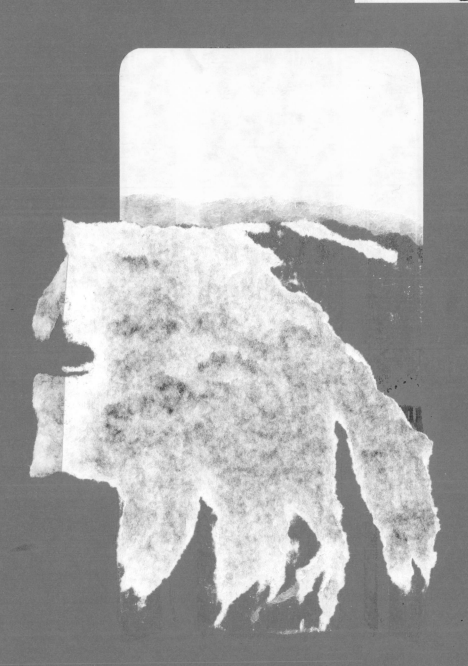

For Duncan

Copyright © 2003 by Scott Beck
All rights reserved.
CIP Data is available.
Published in the United States by Dutton Children's Books,
a division of Penguin Putnam Books for Young Readers
345 Hudson Street, New York, New York 10014
www.penguinputnam.com
Designed by Gloria Cheng
Printed in China
First Edition
1 3 5 7 9 10 8 6 4 2
ISBN 0-525-47040-9

A Mud Pie for Mother

by Scott Beck

DUTTON CHILDREN'S BOOKS • NEW YORK

Little Pig needed something
for Mother Pig's birthday.

I will give this flower to
Mother Pig, he thought.

"That flower is my favorite," buzzed
the bee. "Please don't take it."

"If it is your favorite, then I won't take it," said Little Pig.

"I will take this pretty yellow
hay instead."

"Oh no," mooed the cow.

"That hay is my bed!"

"In that case, I will take these
shiny seeds," grunted Little Pig as
he squeezed under the fence.

"Cluck! Cluck! I was going to eat those," squawked the hen.

"Then I guess I'll just take some dirt and make a mud pie for Mother," Little Pig decided.

Little Pig put back the dirt.
Now he had nothing for Mother Pig.

But then the farmer's wife said, "What a good little pig!" And she gave him some bread.

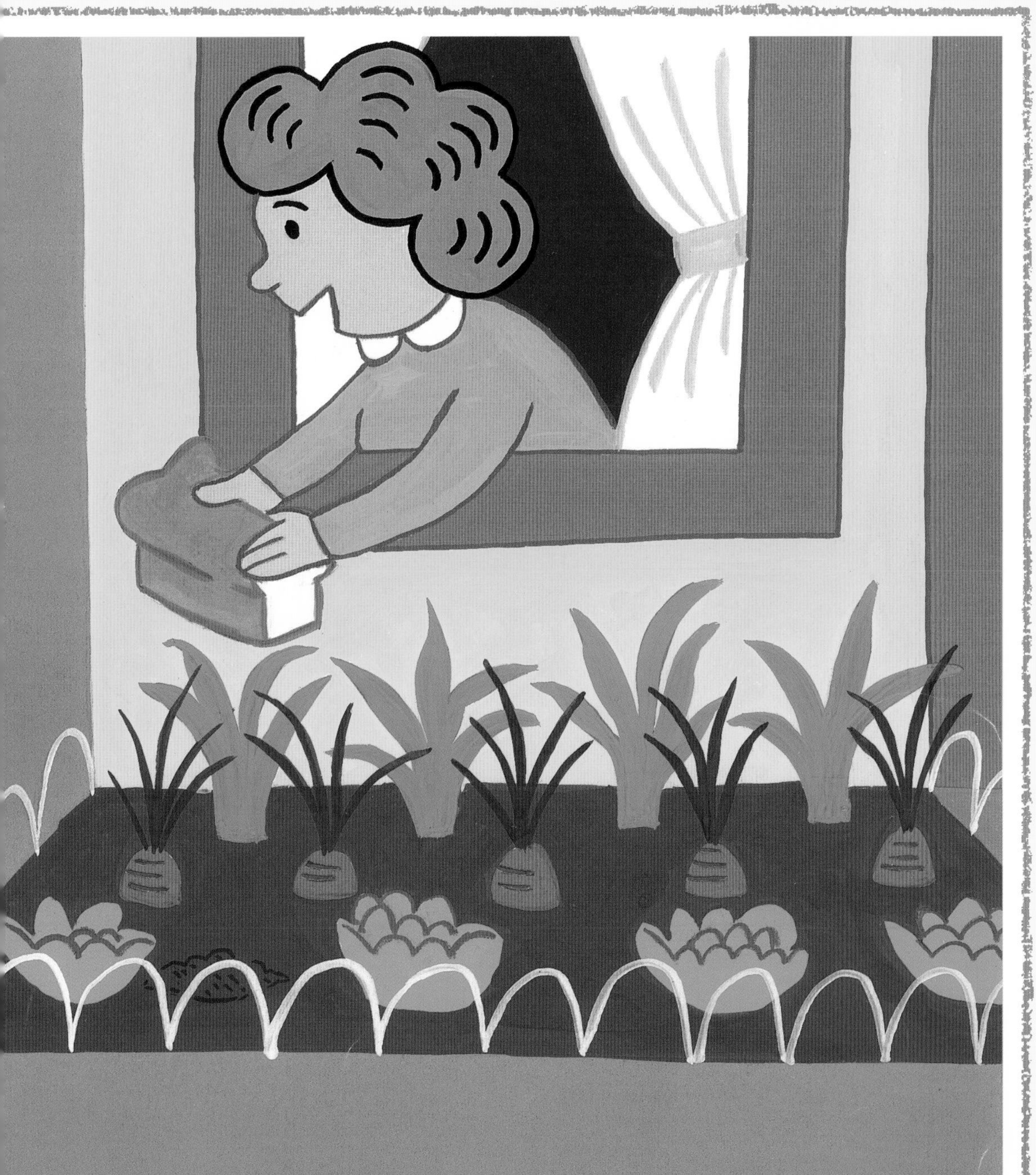

On his way home, the hen said, "Thank you for letting me eat the seeds."

And she gave him some eggs.

Little Pig was so happy he
ran right past the cow.
"Wait," she mooed. "I want to
thank you for not taking the hay."

And she gave him some milk.

Then Little Pig met the bee. "I made honey from the flower," she buzzed. "Please take some—it's very sweet."

So Little Pig took the honey and

the milk and the eggs and the bread...

and he made a big, beautiful
breakfast for Mother Pig's birthday.

Do you know, it was
just what she wanted.